D1164589

Phoebe Gilman

The Blue Hippopotamus

Based on a story by Joan Grant

Illustrated by
Joanne Fitzgerald

North Winds Press
An Imprint of Scholastic Canada Ltd.

This book was created in watercolour, gouache and coloured pencil, on Lanaquarelle 300 lb. Hot Pressed paper.

The type in this book was set in 17 point Nueva.

Library and Archives Canada Cataloguing in Publication
Gilman, Phoebe, 1940-2002.
The blue hippopotamus / Phoebe Gilman ; illustrated by Joanne Fitzgerald.
Based on The blue faience hippopotamus by Joan Grant.
I. Fitzgerald, Joanne, 1956- II. Grant, Joan Marshall, 1907-1989. Blue faience hippopotamus. III. Title.

PS8563.I54B58 2005   jC813'.54   C2005-901010-X

ISBN-13 978-0-439-95260-6
ISBN-10 0-439-95260-3

6 5 4 3 2 1   Printed in Singapore   07 08 09 10 11

For loving hippos everywhere — whether green, brown or blue.
— J. F.

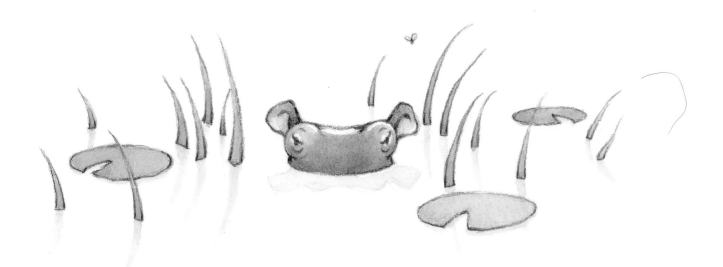

Long, long ago and far away, in the land of the Pharoahs, there lived a little hippopotamus named Hapu. Each day, just as the rays of the sun turned the Nile River to rippling gold, he came down to wallow in the squishy-squashy mud.

One morning, as he nibbled a tasty green reed, he heard the sound of splashing and giggling.

"What's that?" he said, looking about.

It was Mery-Am, the Pharoah's daughter. She was so playful, splashing around in the water and diving off the warm rocks, that the little hippopotamus fell in love.

"I want to play too," he called out, and he swam over to meet her.

"Help! Help!" she screamed, and rushed away.

His friends all laughed at him. "You are very silly, Hapu. A little girl can not play with a hippopotamus."

Hapu sank back down in the mud. "It is true," he said. "She can never love me as I love her."

"Hmm," said a heron who was catching fish nearby. "I wouldn't be too sure of that. Stranger things have happened. I was once a butterfly, but I grew tired of being so little and went to see the great magician who lives in the cave beyond the pyramids. Now see how grand I am."

Hapu rose out of the mud. He wanted to hear more, but the heron flew away.

"Beyond the pyramids," Hapu said. "I have never been that far by myself, but I should be able to get there if I try. Surely, if the magician can change a butterfly into a heron, he can change me into a boy. Then Mery-Am will not be afraid to play with me."

Hapu followed the Nile, past the pyramids, until at last he saw a heron with a very startled look on its face flying out of a cave.

"It might easily have been a butterfly a few minutes ago," thought Hapu.

He peeked into the cave. There was the magician.

"Please, sir," Hapu said. "Would you change me into a prince so that Mery-Am will love me?"

"A human?" said the magician. "No, I can't do that. I have tried that particular magic many times, but I've never been able to get it right. There must be a secret ingredient that I am missing."

A large tear ran out of Hapu's eye and splashed on the floor. He turned to go.

"Wait," said the magician. "There are lots of other things that little girls love. Is she vain? I could turn you into a mirror."

"Oh, no," said Hapu, "not at all vain."

"Is she greedy? I could turn you into a large sausage."

"*Not a sausage*," Hapu said. "Perhaps something to play with. I am too big.
I frighten her."

"Ah! A toy, excellent suggestion," said the magician. "What shape do you prefer?"

"I don't want to sound conceited," said Hapu, "but I think that hippos are really the nicest shape. Too large, perhaps, but a very nice shape."

The magician shook his wand over Hapu's head. *"Sheh-shu, sheh-shu, kalabasha."*

Suddenly the walls of the cave seemed very far away, and the magician very tall.

His voice boomed from far above. "What do you think?"

"Is that really me?" asked the hippopotamus. "I'm blue!"

"Yes, lovely colour, isn't it?" said the magician. "Now I shall find a trader to take you to Mery-Am."

"Suppose she doesn't want me?" whispered Hapu.

"I am certain that she will," said the magician. "But just in case, I have given you one wish. If she doesn't want you, simply say, 'I wish to be a real hippo again.'"

The magician waved his wand and began to sing softly, "*Sheh-shu sheh-shu, sheh-shu-sha,*" and Hapu fell fast asleep.

He awoke just as the trader was lifting him up to show Mery-Am.

"Oh," she said. "Please, please, please may I have him, Father?"

The Pharoah gave the trader two gold coins, and Mery-Am took the toy hippo's string.

"I shall call you Hapu. Follow me, Hapu," she said, and she pulled him round and round. The toy hippo was very happy, even though he did prefer the feel of soft, squelchy mud to the rumble-bumping of wheels.

Wherever Mery-Am went, the toy hippo went too. "Watch me," she called as she dove off the rocks. Then she giggled and splashed him with water. "You shall have a bath, too."

When Mery-Am ate her dinner, Hapu sat beside her plate, and often she fed him honey and sesame cakes.

But as the years passed, Mery-Am began to leave him on the cedar chest next to her bed. Though she remembered to pat him before she went to sleep, for most of the day he was lonely, listening for her footsteps.

One evening, Mery-Am picked him up and stroked him gently. He felt a tear splash on his back. "Dear little hippopotamus," she said. "You are lucky to be made of clay. You don't know what it feels like to be lonely. How I wish my own true love would find me." Then she put him down and blew out her lamp.

Hapu lay awake in the darkness. "I can never be Mery-Am's own true love.
I can not make her happy."

Then he remembered: "I still have my wish."

He thought of basking in the sun and talking to his friends. He could almost

taste the crisp, green plants on his tongue and feel the squishy mud between
his toes. "I could be my old self again, or ..."

He sighed and wished his one wish. "May Mery-Am find her own true love,
and may they live happily ever after."

The next morning a young prince came up-river. Just as the little hippopotamus had done, he fell in love with Mery-Am. And she fell in love with him.

On the day they were married, a careless servant knocked Hapu off the cedar chest. He felt himself falling and closed his eyes as he broke into pieces. "What a curious sensation this breaking apart is," he thought. "I feel quite dizzy and light."

Up and up Hapu drifted like a cloud. Down below, he saw the magician's cave. "I have changed many animals and granted many wishes," said the magician, "but you were the only one to wish unselfishly for another's happiness instead of your own."

Blown by the wind and warmed by the stars, Hapu fell fast asleep. The floods of summer came and went, and still he slept. The fields were sown, the crops were gathered, and still he slept. High above the Earth and out among the stars he slept until, one day, he heard someone calling to him. Hapu awoke and smiled.

Mery-Am smiled back and said, "You are the most beautiful
little baby that ever was born!"